MEMORIALS TO THE MISSING

A Play for Radio

By

STEPHEN WYATT

Copyright Stephen Wyatt 2008
ISBN 978-0-9556868-1-8

All enquiries concerning performance or reproduction rights should be addressed to Valerie Hoskins Associates, 20, Charlotte Street, London W1P IHJ. Telephone – 0207637 4490.

MEMORIALS TO THE MISSING was first broadcast on November 8th 2007.

It was made by PIER PRODUCTIONS for BBC RADIO 4.

The cast –
FABIAN WARE	Anton Lesser
EDWIN LUTYENS	Michael Maloney
GENERAL MACREADY	Keith Drinkel
LADY FLORENCE CECIL	Teresa Gallagher
ALICE / NURSE	Sophie Roberts
FIRST VOICE / JAMES	Karl Davies
SECOND VOICE	Alex Wyndham
THIRD VOICE / AITKEN	Ben Crowe

The play was directed by MARTIN JENKINS

(AFTER TITLES)
(A VOICE READING FROM THE ROLL CALL OF NAMES ON THE MEMORIAL AT THIEPVAL.
(THEN OVER THIS, WHISPERING VOICES:)

ONE: (NORTH COUNTRY) I was sixteen. Lied about my age, didn't I, so I could enlist. Wanted to serve my country. Do what's right. You know, become a hero. Fat chance. Cut to pieces in the first moments of the attack by a burst of machine gun fire.

TWO: (UPPER CLASS) I was twenty-three, just married, first child on the way. Still scrabbling around for a career. But my wife agreed that it was right for me to go. This shell burst – very close - that's all I can remember.

THREE: (COCKNEY) I was thirty almost. Been working on the docks all my life. So I loved the excitement of being abroad and being one of the lads. "Your advance will end the war." That's what they told us. Perhaps it did. I'm not around to know.

ONE: I'm one of the missing.

TWO: I'm one of the missing.

THREE: I'm one of the missing.

(THE VOICE OF THE ROLL CALL CONTINUES UNDER :)

WARE: (V.O.) I do not see myself as a superstitious or overly religious man. But it seems that for most of my later life I have been haunted by these voices – the voices of the dead.

(CROSSFADE INTO BUZZ OF EXPECTANT GUESTS)
(THEN A GAVEL. BANQUET 1932)

TOASTMASTER: My lords, ladies and gentlemen, pray silence for Major General Sir Fabian Ware, CMG, CB, KBE, KCVO.

(HUSH FROM GUESTS AS WARE RISES)

WARE: My lords, ladies and gentlemen, I have been asked tonight to say something of the work of the Imperial War Graves Commission with which I have had the honour to be associated since its inception during the latter days of the Great War. As we know, the losses were and still are almost beyond comprehension. Britain and her Dominions lost 975,399 dead. Many of them in unmarked graves in distant lands or lost for ever in the mud of Flanders. The task of recording their deaths and providing memorials fitting to such loss and such sacrifice has been the guiding principle behind all the Commission's work. Perhaps it's appropriate if I begin by saying something about the origins of the Commission. In the very early days of the War, I was involved in…

(HIS VOICE STARTS TO FADE DURING THIS.)
(TO BE REPLACED AGAIN BY WARE'S INNER VOICE, QUIETER, MORE THOUGHTFUL)

WARE: (V.O.) Speaking of it now it's very easy to make everything seem so planned and so inevitable. So easy to forget about the exhaustion that set in when I was tired of arguing with bone-headed officials. And to ignore the powerful voices who opposed what we were doing. Perhaps it's fortunate that I've always been better at providing solutions than asking questions.

(CUT BACK TO WARE AT THE BANQUET)

WARE: When the Great War began, I was already forty-five. A newspaper editor no longer with a newspaper to edit. I was too old for active service and too young to stay at home and wait. So I volunteered for the ambulance service and was put in charge of the motley collection of private cars and drivers which became known as the Red Cross Mobile Unit. Our job was to search out the wounded and dying and bring them to wherever they could be cared for. But I soon began to feel that part of our work had to involve collecting evidence about the dead – who they were, where they had fallen and where they were being buried.

(ADD IN 1910s TYPE CAR OVER BUMPY ROAD COMING TO A HALT. DISTANT SHELLING).
(CUT TO FEET OVER GROUND. 1914)

WARE: (V.O.) I can still see it. Two small clumps of graves in the fields near Bethune. I was in the vicinity so I went to see what state they were in. There were probably no more than ten graves in all. Lying there among some battered vegetables. With makeshift crosses also battered and broken by the rain.

(AS THE FEET STOP, THE VOICE OF ONE OF THE DEAD - AN UPPER CLASS YOUNG MAN)

JAMES: I was just twenty-one. As I was already at university and good at sports, this meant I was officer material. Became a Second Lieutenant. My men were rough round the edges, ordinary working-class fellows. Never met men like that before. Never talked to them anyway. They were decent enough and willing I'll give them that. Brave too. So when my map-reading got us trapped in enemy fire, they stood their ground. They did their best to give me a decent burial. The ones who were left alive that is.

(FOOTSTEPS APPROACHING OVER FIELD.)

ALICE: (YOUNG, REFINED) Excuse me, sir.

WARE: Of course.

ALICE: I saw you arrive just now, you see, and start to study the graves and I - I'm probably being very foolish

WARE: (POLITELY) I'm sure that's not the case, ma'am.

JAMES: Alice –

ALICE: It's just that the instructions were so very precise. That is Bethune over there, isn't it?

JAMES: (MORE URGENTLY) Alice –

WARE: Forgive me, ma'am, but I confess I'm rather concerned to see you here unaccompanied. This is hardly a place for a young woman to –

ALICE: Please don't concern yourself about that, sir. I have a driver waiting for me over there. My family knows that I am here.

ALICE: I am looking for the grave of my brother, James. Perhaps you know him? Second Lieutenant James Cheveley?

WARE: I'm afraid I never had the honour.

JAMES: I'm here, Alice.

ALICE: I talked to his comrades in his regiment. They were most kind. They gave me the particulars of the exact place where – where James is buried. He died a hero they told me. They even described the temporary wooden cross and the

	inscription they had written upon it. I'm sure they wouldn't deceive me.
WARE:	I'm certain they wouldn't.
ALICE:	I'm glad you confirm my impression. You see, I was looking over there because I thought that was the place they had described. Over there beyond the tree. But now I'm confused.
JAMES:	I'm here, Alice. Remember the gold ring you gave me? I'm still wearing it.
ALICE:	(STRUGGLING) So perhaps they meant here where you are looking.
JAMES:	Look hard, Alice. I am here.
	(PAUSE.)
ALICE:	But no – you can't make out any of the names out here either.
WARE:	Sadly the rain has done its best to obliterate them.
JAMES:	They only had time to write my name and rank but they did their best.
ALICE:	What are these crosses made from?
WARE:	Whatever's to hand. This one looks like an old army ration box to me. And this one – well, it's some kind of shell-case…
ALICE:	And that's it?
JAMES:	They did their best.

ALICE:	He was my only brother and the apple of the eye of my parents. Such a talented young man with a great future. I had so hoped to find the spot where he was buried.
JAMES:	That last afternoon, Alice, remember? When we went for a long walk and talked about all the things we would do, all the places we would visit, when I came home.
ALICE:	Somehow I'd imagined he'd have a proper grave like in the churchyard at home. That was doubtless very foolish of me. But I did think there would be more than – this.
WARE:	We do what we can. But there are so many calls upon our time. I have already made one very simple practical proposal. Every man should be given a well-made cross with a painted inscription and a tarred base to stop the rot so –
ALICE:	<u>(CLOSE TO TEARS)</u> I know I should understand your difficulties but - I cannot. But I'm sure we will find the body in the end. And when it's been located, my family will make arrangements for James to be taken back to England
JAMES:	No, Alice, listen –
ALICE:	He can then be buried appropriately with full honours in the family tomb.

JAMES: Alice, listen, I don't want that. These are my men. We died together. I never thought I'd think that but I do. I don't deserve special treatment. They were decent fellows.

WARE: I am sorry to have disappointed you. But the task is huge. I will try to make further enquiries and see if I can – Cheveley, you said?

ALICE: Oh, I don't blame you. You will probably think me very silly for being upset when I should be proud that he has given his life to defend his country but – but –

JAMES: (SOFTLY) Alice – listen to me.

(BUT HER CONTROL FINALLY GOES)

ALICE: Oh, James, James, where are you?

JAMES: Alice – please –

ALICE: James, James, come back to me.

(HER ANGUISHED CRIES ARE DROWNED OUT BY THE SOUND OF HEAVY SHELL FIRE)
(THEN FADE DOWN UNDER:)

WARE: (V.O.) Was it then the voices first spoke to me? Was it then that I knew it was my responsibility to make sure they were remembered – each and every one of them equal in death? I don't know. In all the books I've ever read and all the pictures I've ever seen when someone has a vision it comes to them in a sudden blinding moment of revelation. Well, that's not been my experience. My vision was built laboriously bit by bit.

(CUT TO A DOOR BURSTING OPEN)

WARE: (ENTERING) General Macready, forgive me.

MACREADY: Good God, man. How dare you –

WARE: Please – forgive me. I need to speak to you personally and your staff have not been co-operative. This was the only way.

(DOOR SHUTS)

MACREADY: You must be Fabian Ware.

WARE: But how did –

MACREADY: (INTERRUPTING) No other civilian would beard a general in his office without an invitation.

WARE: I'm sorry.

MACREADY: I'm afraid your reputation precedes you, sir. Do you seriously imagine that I am here to lend an ear to every bleeding heart who brings me some sorry tale of injustice? Most of us are here to fight a war.

WARE: The successful prosecution of the war is, of course, paramount and –

MACREADY: I'm glad you recognise that.

WARE: And I would be the first to admit that what I have to propose has nothing to do with its successful termination.

MACREADY: Well, that's honest at least. So – why <u>must</u> you see me?

WARE: Put simply, I believe it is vital that the Army maintains a thorough register of every single man who dies in action and ensures that every single grave is clearly marked.

MACREADY: They tell me that once you have a bee in your bonnet there is no stopping you.

WARE: I hope – I believe – this is more than a bee in my bonnet.

MACREADY: Does this mean the Red Cross isn't doing its job?

WARE: The Red Cross is doing a remarkable job in appalling circumstances –

MACREADY: But?

WARE: I believe the Armed Forces have a moral obligation to be involved in this as well. Indeed I think the only possible way to proceed is for the Army to take full responsibility for this work.

(PAUSE)

MACREADY: Very well, Mr Ware. Sit down.

WARE: Thank you.

MACREADY: You have three minutes to tell me why as Adjutant-General of the British Expeditionary Force, I should bother with some scheme or other you've dreamed up which won't help us one jot to beat the Germans.

WARE: Firstly, I have no doubt there are those who think that what I wish to propose is of purely sentimental value. I have to disagree.

MACREADY: Disagree all you like, but, manifestly, it's not going to –

WARE: With respect, General, you gave me three minutes and I hope they are three minutes in which you will listen.

(PAUSE. BUT WARE THEN CONTINUES CALMLY :)

WARE: What I am going to say derives from observation and experience not from fine feelings. As you know, I once edited a popular newspaper so I know what sentimental poppycock can be. God knows I've printed enough of it in my time. But I am convinced that what I am proposing will have an extraordinary moral value to the troops in the field as well as to the relatives and friends of the dead at home.

(PAUSE. HE WARMS TO HIS THEME)

WARE: The soldiers value the fact that my men visit the graves close behind the trenches, fully exposed to shell and rifle fire – and yes, on occasions, they have lost their lives as well. But they have come and they have recorded accurately not only the names of the dead but also the exact place of burial. This has a symbolic value to the soldiers that it is difficult to exaggerate. To do this partially or inefficiently – or worse, not at all - would be tantamount to saying that their lives and their sacrifice have been for nothing and are not worthy of account.

(PAUSE)

MACREADY: Two minutes.

WARE: When the war finally ends, there is no doubt the nation will demand an account from the Government regarding the steps which have been taken to mark and classify all these burial places. You know the state of the battlefields better than I do. Such steps can only be taken at, or soon after, burial.

(PAUSE)

WARE: If the task of recording the precise location of the graves and the men who are buried in them is to be done effectively then I will have to start now and devote myself to it full time. And not only myself. I need a specially dedicated unit of men and vehicles as well as the full backing of the Army. And by full backing I don't just mean moral support -

although that is of course valuable. I mean practical support, financial support.

(RUSTLE OF PAPER)

WARE: The current arrangements lack coherence and consistency. I have therefore worked out a revised preliminary plan of operations. I've divided the ground in allied hands into four areas and wish to allot five men, an officer and four vehicles to each. There must also be adequate back-up staff to handle the registration cards and also to deal with the flood of enquiries about the dead and the missing. I am sure you are aware how pressing and numerous such questions are. Some at least must find their way to your own office.

(PAUSE)

MACREADY: One minute.

WARE: (RUSTLE OF PAPER) This is a preliminary budget which I would like to submit for your inspection. Like all budgets, it's probably better perused at leisure, I do not wish to encroach further upon your time than my allotted three minutes. Indeed, if my arguments carry no weight with you, you could listen to me for three hours and my case would not impress you.

MACREADY: Indeed. Is that it?

(PAUSE)

MACREADY: Of course I could kill your proposal stone dead at this very moment.

WARE: I don't think you will.

MACREADY: Oh. And what makes you so confident Mr Ware?

WARE: You served in the Boer War. You know how much distress was caused there by the neglect of the graves and the failure of the Army to chronicle their locations in a proper and acceptable manner. You were a staff officer then.

MACREADY: You've done your research.

WARE: I'm an old newspaper man, remember? My paper published a great deal of very heated, highly critical correspondence. Many felt very bitter about how cavalierly the dead had been treated.

(PAUSE)

MACREADY: You are right, Mr Ware. There was a huge loss of military morale. And a great deal of distress and anger among bereaved relatives. I wouldn't want that to be repeated here –

WARE: Which will be on a much greater scale – given the losses so far – and this time many of the men are volunteers.

MACREADY: (QUIETLY) Just so.

(PAUSE)

MACREADY: You've made your point. But a word of warning. If, as you propose, this should become a military matter then you cannot be allowed to go your own sweet way. You'll find the Army has its own way of doing things.

WARE: It wouldn't be the Army if it didn't. But – with due respect - when it comes to the treatment of men killed in conflict those traditions are hardly glorious. After the glorious victory of Waterloo –

MACREADY: Yes, I know – after Waterloo, the bodies of the officers were taken home but the bodies of the ordinary soldiers were shovelled into large pits in the ground without either ceremony or recognition.

(PAUSE)

WARE: All the men fighting here deserve more and - above all - deserve to be treated equally.

MACREADY: I agree they deserve more. Equally is another matter. The Army is not an egalitarian organisation. The bodies of the officers have always gone home to their family mausoleums. You're never going to change that.

WARE: But this is not a war like any other. You and I know there's a new spirit abroad. The officers I've talked to have said they wish to be buried with their men.

MACREADY: The officers who talk to you are self-selecting. You can't fight military traditions.

WARE: Maybe not. But perhaps I can change them.

(CUT BACK TO WARE AT THE BANQUET)

WARE: In February 1916 the new organisation was named the Directorate of Graves Registration and our officers received commissions. I myself was proud to be made a Lieutenant-Colonel. By May we had registered over 50,000 graves, answered 5,000 enquiries, supplied 2,500 photographs and provisionally selected the sites for about 200 cemeteries. But, of course, we had no idea of the carnage which lay ahead. On the first day of the Battle of the Somme, British casualties alone amounted to mote than 59, 000, over 19,000 of those dead. Many of them missing in action.

(THE VOICES OF THE MISSING RETURN:)

ONE: I was sixteen. I was homesick and dead scared but I didn't want to show it. Zero hour was 7.30 a.m. I had my dad's old compass in my pocket. Sort of mascot I suppose. Sergeant lined us up – and we all had a tot of rum. Not used to it even after all those cold mornings. Everything went blurry. Then the whistles went. Then a blank.

THREE:	I was thirty almost. I had a letter from my girlfriend. Well, I called her that because I loved her. But she was my best mate's wife. Things got difficult – one reason I had to get away. She wrote that she loved me and I kissed her letter – then we went over the top. We were going to score a famous victory. Or so we were told.
TWO:	I was twenty-three, not long married. We were naïve and things weren't too good between us. But my wife gave me a volume of Shelley's poetry to take with me. She knew I loved his work. I tried to read <u>Adonais</u> the night before the attack but couldn't take the words in. Doesn't matter now – does it?
	(SOUNDS OF GUNFIRE.)
WARE:	(V.0.) We became detectives. Bodies destroyed beyond all recognition by the enemy's fire. Corpses disappeared into the mud. Identity discs rotted to mush or nothing. After all, bringing a dead body back from no man's land could hardly be a high priority for anyone. So often all we had were tiny battered relics scooped from the mud. Our only clues to lives destroyed for ever.
	(OPEN AIR ACOUSTIC. FEET OVER MUD)
WARE:	This way, nurse.

NURSE: It's very good of you, General. I know it's bending the rules. But my aunt and uncle are that worried about my cousin, he's missing in action and –

WARE: I understand, nurse. But I respect your work and I couldn't refuse your request. Besides, I know you've seen enough not to be shocked by what's here. I only wish I could hold out some hope. But at least you'll be able to see for yourself the scale of the problem.

(THE FEET STOP)

WARE: These are some of the things which have been retrieved from the trenches.

(A CLINK OF METAL)

WARE: A compass for instance. It survived the shells which reduced its poor owner to pulp.

ONE: (SOFTLY) That's my compass.

WARE: Not much damage. Can you make out the initials? You've younger eyes that mine. Looks like it could be C.E.S.

ONE: C.E.B.

NURSE: No, C.E.B. I think.

ONE: My dad's initials.

NURSE: Well, it's a start, I suppose.

WARE: Yes. So then we have to look under B in the Missing List. But unfortunately there are over twelve thousand B's. If it was C.E.X. we might be in with a chance.

NURSE: But not that many will have the first initials C.E.

ONE: But they're my dad's names not mine. He's Charles Edward. I'm Frederick Ernest.

WARE: Well, my men will give it a try. But what about this? What can this tell you?

(THE NURSE RIFFLES THROUGH PAGES OF BOOK)

NURSE: The Poetical Works of Shelley. I'm afraid I don't know much about poetry.

WARE: Not required. Any name in the front?

TWO: Yes. Yes, there is. Mine – and my address. And a loving inscription from my wife. To help me forget the angry words we'd had before

NURSE: It's hard to tell. Blood must have seeped through into the knapsack. Just a moment – there's something.

TWO: For my dearest husband, Anthony Gilbert Clarke. From his loving wife, Agnes.

WARE: Can you make it out?

NURSE: I'm trying. Looks like "For my dearest…" But the name's all but obliterated.

TWO: "For my dearest husband, Anthony Gilbert Clarke. From his loving wife, Agnes."

NURSE: No, it's hopeless.

WARE: Pity. Believe me, I wish we could trace your cousin but it's against the odds. We've more to go on with these than most.

NURSE: I understand.

TWO: But Agnes will never know. Please –

(A KITBAG PRODUCED)

WARE: Well, perhaps you could turn your sharp young eyes on this.

NURSE: Well, it's just the remains of a pack. A few odd fragments. Cloth. A few bits of bone. Oh, and a fragment of a letter. I can't make anything out.

THREE: Annie's letter! If they read that, they'll know about us. Maybe Bob'll find out – can be violent can Bob –

WARE: Try.

NURSE: "My dear"…

THREE: Can you see? Can you read? It's trouble but at least I'll be remembered.

NURSE: No, I'm sorry, it's hopeless.

THREE: So Annie will always wonder.

WARE: (SIGHING) Another one to add to the list of 'killed in action, no known grave." You see - ?

NURSE: I've dealt with the wounded and the dying. But this – I'd no idea.

WARE: If we can find what's happened to your cousin, we'll tell you. But –

NURSE: You don't hold out any hope?

WARE: Not much, I'm afraid.

(THE OVERLAPPING VOICES CONTINUE)

THREE: Please – don't stop –

ONE: Keep looking –

THREE: For Annie's sake –

TWO: For Agnes –

ONE: For my mam and dad –

(CROSSFADE BACK TO THE BANQUET. THE GUESTS ARE CHUCKLING APPRECIATIVELY)

WARE: No, no, it has been said that I am a difficult man to argue with. I do not feel that is quite fair. I have always been willing to listen to what others have to say. But they had better have good reasons for saying it.

(SOME MORE LAUGHTER. WARE SWITCHES TONE)

WARE: Finally, however, in May 1917 a Royal Charter brought the Imperial War Graves Commission into being. The Commission was charged with caring for the graves of all the members of the Imperial Forces who had died on active service whether on land or sea. It was given the power to acquire land to create cemeteries and permanent memorials outside them. It also had to provide for burials. It had to build and look after memorials. It had to keep records and registers of the graves. It was further charged with honouring and perpetuating the memory of the common sacrifice made by the soldiers of the Empire.

(PAUSE)

WARE: It was also the first organisation ever to be given responsibility for all the dead of a nation in any war. Then, of course, in November 1918 the war ended and –

(HIS SPEECH FADES DOWN UNDER:)

WARE:	(V.O.) And in some ways my own battles truly began. I had the vision – I knew what needed to be done but not how to achieve it. I needed architects and I acquired them – two men who had worked together - Edwin Lutyens and Herbert Baker – but who were in so many ways - chalk and cheese. And when you mixed in Aitken from the National Gallery of British Art it was a pretty combustible combination.
	(CUT TO CAR OVER ROUGH GROUND.) (A SQUEAL OF TYRES AS THE VEHICLE BRAKES)
LUTYENS:	Oops! Bumpsadaisy! Tyres must be tiring.
	(THE CAR STOPS ABRUPTLY)
LUTYENS:	And now we have come to a full stop – as the sentence said. (PAUSE) Stirred but not shaken, eh, Baker?
BAKER:	(STIFFLY) I am fine thank you, Lutyens.
LUTYENS:	And Aitken – I trust you're not aching?
AITKEN:	There is no cause for concern.
WARE:	Shall we proceed, gentlemen?
	(CAR DOORS OPEN. FOOTSTEPS OVER GROUND. BIRDSONG)
WARE:	Some of the heaviest losses during the Battle of the Somme were suffered here.

LUTYENS: What humanity can endure and suffer is beyond belief. But at least there are the poppies growing. Look – Baker – over there, clinging round an exploded shell.

BAKER: (IMPATIENTLY) Yes, yes. But we have more important matters to consider.

LUTYENS: (LISTENING TO BIRDSONG) You know I could have sworn that was a blackbird but I think I'm wrong. What do you think, Baker?

BAKER: I think we should get on with the job in hand. God know it's big enough.

AITKEN: I can but agree, Mr Baker.

(THEY WALK ON)

AITKEN: I believe we must now call you Major-General Ware. My congratulations.

BAKER: And mine.

WARE: Thank you. I am very honoured.

LUTYENS: I should think you must feel burdened too, Mon General. What to do for all these dead boys.

WARE: Which is why I seek for advice.

BAKER: Now it is no secret that Lutyens and I often disagree.

LUTYENS: Oh, I have to disagree.

BAKER:	Very amusing but in this case, our priorities are clear. I confess that my ideas tend more towards the direct and straightforward in terms of sentiment. He prefers the abstract and monumental.
LUTYENS:	You make it sound like a crime.
BAKER:	The fact is – in this case, there is no place for your sort of grandiosity.
LUTYENS:	(LISTENING) No, I'm wrong, it is a blackbird.
AITKEN:	If I might interject, gentlemen? I am of the opinion that we must not get carried away. In the present post-war climate, it would be criminal to spend vast sums of money on useless structures however decorative. Far better to have something simple - of modest cost.
LUTYENS:	(LISTENING) And there's its mate.
AITKEN:	Far better to spend money on housing or something useful. Personally I think the most valuable memorial would be some sort of national university, something which has practical value, not an empty monument to what cannot be brought back.
LUTYENS:	Oh no, nothing practical. Nothing practical at all.
AITKEN:	Why ever not?

LUTYENS: Because – because in the end they cease to be monuments. They become universities or hospitals or public conveniences and people forget why they are there. The missing will go missing yet again.

BAKER: So what are you proposing?

LUTYENS: My dear Baker, if there is to be a national university, let there be one. But if it is pretending to be a memorial to those who lie around us here under the earth then – for once – greedy though I am for work - I would not challenge your right to be its architect. (LISTENING) Ah, they've found each other.

BAKER: Lutyens, I know your tactics. Don't expect me to be put out by them.

AITKEN: With all due respect to you both, gentleman, we must not get carried away with dreams. All we need are simple respectful cemeteries each one responding to the particular nature of where it is and who is buried there. All that is needed then is a simple cross.

BAKER: Well, I think the dead deserve more than that. But I agree with you about crosses. In fact, I have already in mind a design for a cross which I think will –

LUTYENS: Oh no, no crosses.

BAKER: No crosses! Good God man, we are a Christian country which has fought a just Christian war and the consolation of the cross is what our soldiers would look to. Certainly what sustains their grieving relatives.

LUTYENS: And the Muslims who fought and hate the idea of having bodies exhumed? And the Hindus who prefer cremation to burial. And the Chinese who –

AITKEN: Let them have their burial places according to their own rituals. And let the Christians have theirs. We are the majority after all.

LUTYENS: I'm sorry, it just won't do.

BAKER: Lutyens, you are impossible. You'll be telling me next that everybody, officer or private, religious or irreligious, regardless of the wishes of their families, should be buried cheek by jowl in the same place.

LUTYENS: The thought had entered my mind. If you consider the tenets of Theosophy for example they are based upon the belief that religion is universal not specific and that ultimately all faiths are the same faith. There is something to be said for the notion.

BAKER: Not a great deal. Unless, like you, you happen to married to a woman who believes in such airy-fairy nonsense.

LUTYENS: Baker, even by your standards, that is quite exceptionally rude.

BAKER: I apologise. But — well - sometimes you provoke me. (PAUSE) Major-General Ware, excuse me –

AITKEN: Mr Baker, I'll come with you. I do not altogether despair of you coming round to my point of view. Unlike Mr Lutyens.

(FOOTSTEPS WALKING AWAY)

LUTYENS: As you must be aware, Baker and I resemble a sort of architectural Punch and Judy show. But that presumably is why you've brought us both here.

WARE: And Mr Aitken?

LUTYENS: Poor chap – so totally wrong. Ever since I saw my first sad little gathering of war graves, I have known that.

(PAUSE)

LUTYENS: My wife has embraced the faith of Theosophy and believes all truth lies in the soul of a rather beautiful young Indian man. But I choose to believe there is something valuable in what she has to say. No, that's less than fair. I do believe that we have to rise above the notion that one faith or one nation has the monopoly of truth. What we do here must transcend all that. Do you agree?

(PAUSE)

WARE: All I know for certain is that the world – our world - has changed for ever. There's no point in pretending we can go back. We have to build buildings which are in some way truthful. But what does Major-General Ware know? Major-General Ware! I feel a fraud.

LUTYENS: You're not a fraud. You're an honest man. And that counts for a great deal.

WARE: (QUIETLY) Thank you.

(PAUSE. BIRDSONG)

LUTYENS: Look – they are flying off together.

(PAUSE)

LUTYENS: Crosses are all very well. And Baker will design a very decent cross. But I look here and I think –

(SUDDENLY THE VOICES)

ONE: You think?

TWO: What do you think?

THREE: Tell us what you think.

ONE: We need to know.

TWO: We have to hear.

(PAUSE)

LUTYENS: Tell me first, General Ware and Whyfor – is everybody the same?

WARE: No.

LUTYENS: But how do they differ? Class? Wealth? Religion? Education?

WARE: They are all individuals.

LUTYENS: And here we have hundreds of thousands of individuals who died in a very anonymous way. Does the class matter? Does the religion matter? Does the education matter?

(PAUSE)

LUTYENS: So this is our fate. Our fate accompli. We are the middle-aged men who have been charged by destiny with commemorating the deaths of thousands of decent people for – for what?

(PAUSE)

LUTYENS: Nobody has ever built monuments to failure. They build triumphal arches to celebrate victories – that is what history tells us. Well, yes, we did indeed win. But at what cost? I don't think you can – or should - celebrate destruction on such a huge scale. And there are those in their graves and those who are missing and we have to serve both.

WARE: I am a practical man. I have been guided throughout by a notion of doing right by all those who died. But I don't have a vision. I don't *see* what should be here. You do.

(PAUSE)

ONE: Tell us.

TWO: Tell us how we will be remembered.

THREE: Tell us what you see.

(PAUSE)

LUTYENS: There are many people besides Baker who think that there should be crosses here. And weeping angels. And mourning classical figures gathered in decorative groups. You could save yourself a great deal of trouble by listening to them rather than to me.

WARE: I've not come all this way to save myself trouble when I'm this close to my goal.

LUTYENS: You are determined, aren't you? I like that. Well, anyway, crosses. They make me cross. Immediately you exclude men of other faiths who've died here. And there's even a practical consideration which may come in useful later on.

WARE: Anything which would impress a committee.

LUTYENS: Ah, a committee! Well, if you think about it, you can't get much information on a cross. So if you want to record somebody's name, rank, regiment, religion, age, and perhaps an appropriate quotation selected by the family, you can't do it. Point one for your committee.

(PAUSE)

LUTYENS: Point two - what I see are - headstones. Rows of them of uniform height and width with a curved top and straight sides. Arranged almost like serried ranks of troops on perpetual parade. But each with the possibility that it can be individualised and the particular soldier remembered. Name, rank, religion, all that should be said.

WARE: (MOVED) Yes, that's how it should be.

LUTYENS: Must be Portland stone. Nothing else is good enough. Point three. All around - trees, grass, foliage. A very English landscape. Point four – there has to be a focal point - a structure – in every cemetery - something which – which –

(PAUSE)

LUTYENS: I'm afraid I can only call it an altar.

WARE: A Christian altar?

LUTYENS: No! No! Not because I have any disrespect for the faith in which I was born. But as we've already agreed this is not about a particular religion, it's about thousands of individuals – and it's also about proportions. I see a stone twelve foot long reached by a platform of three steps. The stone is a section of a vast circle. In fact, the stone has a secret geometrical meaning. It is part of an

	unseen circle, it is a symbol of completion, of sacrifice.
	(PAUSE).
LUTYENS:	Theosophy may have rotted my brain. Maybe you'll want to alter my altar.
	(HE STARTS TO CRY)
LUTYENS:	I'm sorry.
WARE:	Why should you be? There is so much waste, so much desolation here.
LUTYENS:	At least Mr Blackbird and his wife are alive and well.
WARE:	(GENTLY) So – what should be written on this stone? Should anything be written?
LUTYENS:	Let's ask Kipling. I know he will understand.
	(CUT TO THE SOUNDS OF A BUSY MALE CLUB) (THE RUSTLE OF PAPER.)
LUTYENS:	Well, here are Kipling's proposals. So it seems appropriate to discuss them in the midst of the Establishment surrounded by Bishops, Generals and Admirals. They're very good.
WARE:	Kipling lost his son, didn't he?

LUTYENS: Yes but he doesn't talk about it. Thinks it's wrong to claim any special status for himself. What I like about his suggestions is that he has understood what my fellow club members would detest. So I'd better keep my voice down. (SOTTOVOCE) "All are equal under God." For my unalterable altar he is proposing a quotation from the Book of Ecclesiastes - "Their Name Liveth for Evermore". And for those headstones where the name of the dead man is not known, he suggests a phrase of his own devising. "A Soldier of the Great War– Known unto God".

(A COUGH)

MACREADY: Gentlemen, if I might interrupt you for a moment.

WARE: General Macready – please join us.

MACREADY: No, I won't. I just wanted to say a few brief words.

LUTYENS: Of course, but –

MACREADY: Sir Edwin - as we must now call you – as Major-General Ware – as I must now call him – knows - I was instrumental in beginning the whole process of planning the Imperial War Graves Commission. I played only a small part –

WARE: But a crucial one.

MACREADY: I believed in what you asked for and so I helped you achieve it. But I have to warn you that opinion is turning against you. Warned you when we first met and I warn you again now.

LUTYENS: Believe me, General, in everything we propose, there is underlying an enormous respect for the traditions of the Armed Forces. The men will be buried according to their regiments and –

MACREADY: But the officers should not be buried with the men. What is the point of speaking of tradition if you deliberately ignore such a fundamental principle? And as for the traditions of the Church –

LUTYENS: Buried in the ground will be Jews, Muslims, Hindus and men of other creeds. I truly believe they are equal before God.

MACREADY: But with due respect, you are not a regular church-goer. Nor is Mr Rudyard Kipling who is, I believe, advising you. Nor, General Ware, are you.

WARE: Does that make us irreligious men?

MACREADY: It certainly makes you unrepresentative of the majority of the people of this country and disrespectful of its Anglican traditions. There - said what I meant to say. And please take this as a friendly warning. Good afternoon, gentlemen.

(PAUSE. NOTICEABLY QUIETER ATMOSPHERE IN CLUB AS HE WALKS AWAY)

LUTYENS: Oh dear.

WARE: Well, now I know we have a fight on our hands.

(THE CLUB SOUNDS FADE.)
(CUT TO DOOR OPENING. WARE ENTERS)

LADY FLORENCE: (RISING) General Ware –

WARE: (STARTLED) I'm sorry, but –

LADY F: Lady Florence Cecil, wife of the Bishop of Exeter.

WARE: Of course, please be seated.

(THEY BOTH SIT)

LADY F: I apologise for my insistence on seeing you personally.

WARE: Not at all. Would you care for some refreshment? Tea perhaps?

LADY F: General Ware, I think you know why I am here.

WARE: I have of course read the correspondence which you –

LADY F: To which, if I may say so, you do not seem to pay sufficient attention.

WARE: I have tried. I know you feel strongly about these matters and –

LADY F: That is why I have appealed to the Prince of Wales as President of the War Graves Commission. This tyranny has to stop.

WARE: Lady Cecil –

LADY F: I'm sorry, there is no other word for it. Tell me, General, did you lose any sons in this war?

WARE: No, I did not.

LADY F: I lost three. Three brave handsome sons. The pain and the loss are more than somebody in your fortunate position can possibly imagine. There is not a day – a night – when I do not grieve for my boys.

WARE: Of course, I understand.

LADY F: No, General, I don't think you do. What do you suppose has sustained me and my husband during these dark hours? The only thing which has sustained us? It is the hope of the cross. The belief that because of Christ's sacrifice, I will indeed be united with my three lovely boys in Heaven. It is only through that hope that I – and many like me – have been able to carry on the life from which all sunshine seems to have gone.

WARE: I don't wish to deny –

LADY F: For the War Graves Commission to seek to deny us the emblem of our hope and our faith adds heavily to our sorrow. I am not just speaking for myself. I speak in the name of thousands of heartbroken parents –

WARE: I appreciate –

LADY F: No, General, you do not appreciate. Nor do you begin to understand. How could you? For you and your Commission, this is all about finding a solution. You forget that the dead were once flesh and blood-

WARE: But that is –

LADY F: How can you refuse to listen to us? How can you deny the bereaved any say in regard to the graves of their loved ones? We have accepted that our sons will not be brought home. We have understood why that should be. But by what right have you and your collaborators decided that our views and our beliefs are worthless?

WARE: Lady Cecil, of course your beliefs are not worthless.

LADY F: Are I supposed to be grateful for that crumb? Perhaps I should put the question more simply. Are we to be denied the right to commemorate our boys according to our beliefs, however quaint they may appear to you?

WARE: Lady Cecil, if memorials were allowed to be erected in the War Cemeteries according to the preference, taste and means of relatives and friends, what would be the result? Consider how the costly monuments put up by the well-to-do over their dead would contrast unkindly with those humbler ones which would be all that poorer folk could afford. Can that be right - when all the men who fought and died side by side did so for a common cause?

(PAUSE)

LADY F: General Ware, I need no lectures from you on caring for the poor. Or for the charity and respect which should be shown them. But the society you are describing is one without distinction of birth, class or intelligence. Are you saying that I am not allowed to do the best I can for my three brave dead boys?

WARE: I do not wish for a moment to deny the importance of your sacrifice or the devastation of your grief. But our mission is to commemorate all the dead, whatever their social position, whatever their religion or race, whether their final resting place is known or whether their remains lie unidentified in mountains of mud.

(PAUSE)

LADY F:	(RISING) I think there is no longer any point in continuing this conversation. Our only resource is to pursue this matter in Parliament. I bid you good morning.
	(PAUSE. SHE LEAVES. A DOOR SLAMS.) (A SIGH FROM WARE)
WARE:	(V.O.) Why couldn't they understand?
ONE:	I wonder what my mam is doing now? Bet she's crying. But bet she's proud of me too. She'll want to think I didn't die for nothing. Better still - tell herself I'm a hero. But what can I tell her? What answer can anyone give her? Mam and dad haven't two pennies to rub together – and they'll miss the money I should be bringing in.
THREE:	Here under the ground there's a lot of lads like me. Wet about the ears. Wanting to do their bit. Fight for King and Country. Dead by our thousands and missing in action.
WARE:	(V.O.) I know, I know. But it has to be one thing at a time. One boulder pushed up the hill before we attempt another.
	(CUT TO EXTERIOR – GARDEN) (LUTYENS AND WARE WALKING)
LUTYENS:	I think in one way, we are alike, Mon General. We are – and are not – members of the Establishment. And when they don't like something, they try to stamp it out.

WARE: But we're not giving in.

LUTYENS: Did I say we were? But remember, there's a great deal of money involved and a bevy of bishops and garrison of garrumphing generals on the warpath.

WARE: Well, there's no doubt now there'll be a debate in the House, Royal Charter or no Royal Charter. They could easily starve the Commission of the money if they chose to.

LUTYENS: Oh yes, there'll be a few M.P.s bewailing the fact that the money could have been spent on schools and hospitals instead. But I'll wager nobody mentions the fact that the money we need is but a fraction of the money poured into all those futile battles on the Western front.

WARE: The Prime Minister is apparently backing a debate.

LUTYENS: Oh, he always gives in to pressure from the rich and powerful.

WARE: The absence of crosses stands heavily against us with these people.

LUTYENS: Well, there we do have an answer. For all his faults, my old sparring partner, Baker has come up with a perfectly respectable design for a cross. So if I agree to that, he won't oppose my unalterable altar. He's already conceded the headstones.

WARE: I was worrying more about the views of the Church.

LUTYENS: Well, in turmoil as usual. And – again as usual – the Archbishop of Canterbury is sitting on the fence.

(CUT BACK TO BANQUET)

WARE: It is no secret that after the war there was considerable opposition to our work from certain powerful and influential groups. Whether they represented the feeling of the nation in general I will leave you to judge. But in the meantime we had to go through the ordeal of a debate in the House.

(KNOWING LAUGHTER)

WARE: We were in an awkward position. Our opponents could lobby as freely as they wished. But ours was a publicly constituted body and we could not resort to petitions and lobbying. We were therefore fortunate to find a powerful advocate in William Burdett Coutts, the Honourable Member for Westminster…

(CROSSFADE TO EXPECTANT BUZZ IN PARLIAMENT)
(CUT TO BURDETT-COUTTS SPEAKING)

COUTTS: This war has seen terrible losses which have affected all of us, but the strange genius of this war is that it has fused and welded into one, without distinction of race, colour or creed, men from all over the Empire who were ready to die for one common cause that they all understood.

(AS COUTTS SPEAKS, WE CROSSFADE BACK TO THE BANQUET AND WARE QUOTING FROM COUTTS' SPEECH. FOR THE FIRST TIME WARE'S VOICE SOUNDS EMOTIONAL)

WARE: He went on to say – "It is that great union, both in action and in death, that the Commissioners seek nobly to commemorate and make perpetual by its policy in design. When soldiers have been asked to comment upon the Commission's proposals, the uniformity of design was what appealed most strongly to all. That the fellowship of War should be perpetuated in death was the unanimous and emphatic desire of everyone, officer and man."

(THERE IS HUSHED SILENCE. (WARE GIVES A SLIGHTLY EMBARRASSED COUGH AND RETURNS TO HIS MORE OFFICIAL TONE)

WARE: I am happy to say Mr Burdett Coutts succeeded beyond all expectation. Of course, there were many other skirmishes with our opponents before our guiding principles were finally accepted but thankfully, they were. And so the Commission has been able to continue with its work to this day.

(APPLAUSE)

WARE: Many cemeteries in different lands designed by different architects have been built all over the world. The headstones recall the names of the men whose bodies have been found and identified. But there remained the hundreds and thousands whom we have simply called the Missing.

ONE: Us.

THREE: All of us.

TWO: Bodies lost and destroyed beneath the earth or buried in an un-named grave.

(BACK TO WARE AT THE BANQUET)

WARE: What should be done for them has always been in the Commission's mind. The idea of empty graves with names on them seemed repellent. And today we see what I can only describe as the supreme expression of the Commission's work – the completion of Sir Edwin Lutyens' Memorial to the Missing of the Somme here in Thiepval.

(CUT TO LUTYENS IN GARDEN CHATTING)

LUTYENS: General Why and Warefore, don't ask me to describe it. I designed it. What is it? It's arches upon arches, all part of one great arch, tunnels of arches running in both directions, it's - it's what it is. And there are walls of Portland stone and on them the names of the 73,357 missing men of the Somme…

(THE ROLL OF HONOUR STARTS AGAIN)
(WARE AT BANQUET)

WARE: Our work has occupied many years and many people. I can understand why there's a feeling in the air that it's time to move on. Why bury ourselves in the past? Can't we move on? I don't believe – and have never believed – that any nation can ever move on unless it has paid its respects to all those who died on its – on our behalf.

(THE ROLL CALL CONTINUE:)

ONE: My mam and dad finally made it to visit me. My mam could barely walk but they managed somehow. They wept when they saw my name on the memorial. And that's not all. Years later a young woman brought her children. Seems she was my great niece or something. She put her hands over where my name is and - cried. Course she couldn't explain to the kids why.

(PAUSE)

TWO: My wife, Agnes, came here every year, sometimes alone, sometimes with the son I never knew. Until she got too frail. She always read some lines of Shelley from my favourite poem – <u>Adonais</u> –
"Alas! That all we loved of him should be,
But for our grief, as if it had not been,
And grief itself be mortal."

(PAUSE)

THREE: I remain a name on a wall in a monument. Nobody's ever visited me. The only person I really cared for was married to someone else and I'm sure she soon forgot me. I'm just a memory. Except a few weeks ago a sergeant in today's army brought his squaddies along. And they looked and they stared and they felt uncomfortable faced with where their own lives might end. But at least they understood something about duty and service. One of them even read my name out loud. I wonder which war he was off to fight in.

(THE ROLL OF HONOUR CONTINUES.
THE PRIVATE VOICE OF WARE ONE MORE TIME -)

WARE: (V.O.) Well, have you been heard? Are you finally at peace?

(THE VOICES FADE.)